The Gingerbread Man

retold by Brenda Parkes and Judith Smith
illustrated by Jacqueline Rogers

Once upon a time,
there was a little old man
　　　and a little old woman.
One day they decided
to bake some gingerbread.

First the little old woman got
some flour and some sugar
some ginger and some butter
and some milk.

Next she got a bowl
and a spoon
and a cup.
She measured and she mixed.

Then she made a Gingerbread Man.
He had a head and a body,

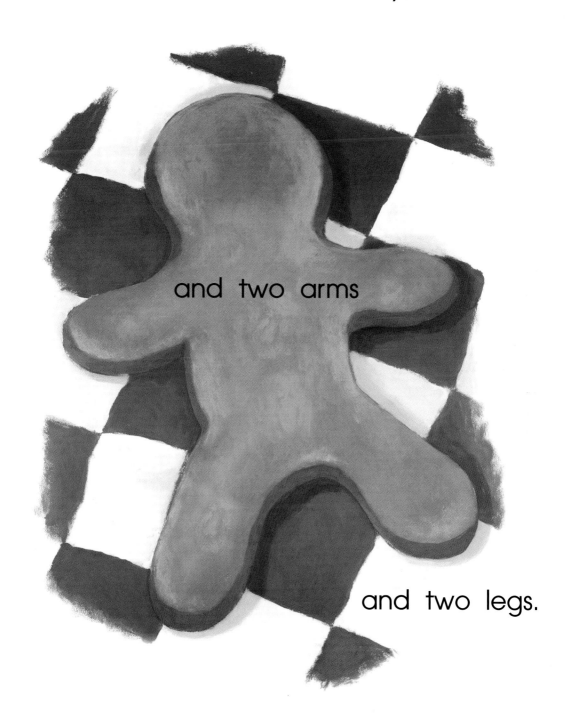

and two arms

and two legs.

The old woman gave him

 2 raisins for his eyes

1 currant for his nose

some peel for his mouth

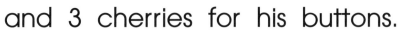 and 3 cherries for his buttons.

Then the old woman put
the Gingerbread Man
into the oven to bake.

Soon the little old man
and the little old woman
smelled the gingerbread cooking.
"Mmmm," said the little old man.
"That smells good. Is it ready to eat?"
"Soon," said the little old woman.

But the little old man was hungry.
So he opened the oven door.

Out jumped the Gingerbread Man.

He ran through the door and

down

the

steps.

"**Stop!**" cried the little old man.
"**Stop!**" cried the little old woman.
But the Gingerbread Man ran **faster**
and **FASTER**.

As he ran, he called,
Run, run, as fast as you can.
You can't catch me,
I'm the Gingerbread Man.
The little old man and woman
both ran after him.

The Gingerbread Man ran
past a boy and a girl.
"**Stop!**" cried the boy.
"**Stop!**" cried the girl.
But the Gingerbread Man ran **faster**
and **FASTER**.

As he ran, he called,
  Run, run, as fast as you can.
  You can't catch me,
  I'm the Gingerbread Man.
The little old man and woman,
  the boy and the girl,
    all ran after him.

The Gingerbread Man ran past
a dog and a cat.
"**Stop!**" barked the dog.
"**Stop!**" meowed the cat.
But the Gingerbread Man ran **faster**
and **FASTER**.

As he ran, he called,
Run, run, as fast as you can.
You can't catch me,
I'm the Gingerbread Man.
The little old man and woman,
the boy and the girl,
the dog and the cat,
all ran after him.

The Gingerbread Man ran on and on, past houses and trees.

He ran up hills and he ran down hills.

Until suddenly, he came to a wide river.
"What am I going to do?" he cried.

The little old man and woman,
the boy and the girl,
the cat and the dog,
all came **closer**
and **CLOSER**.

19

Then along came a fox.
"Don't worry," he said.
"I'll carry you over the river."

"Thank you," said the Gingerbread Man.
And he climbed on to the fox's back.
"Hold on tight," said the fox.
The Gingerbread Man held on tightly.
The fox swam and swam.

Suddenly the Gingerbread Man said,
"Help! My feet are getting wet. I'll melt."

"Climb on to my head," said the fox.

But soon the Gingerbread Man said,
"Help! My body's getting wet. I'll melt."

"Climb out on to my nose," said the fox.
So the Gingerbread Man climbed
out on to the fox's nose.

SNIP

   SNAP!

The fox gobbled up
the Gingerbread Man in one bite.

THE END